JAMESTOWN SETTLEMENT

DISNEP'S
POCAHONTAS

On the High Seas

by Page McBrier

Illustrations by David McCamley, Gillian Coughlan,
Lureline Kohler and D. Blakely Fuller

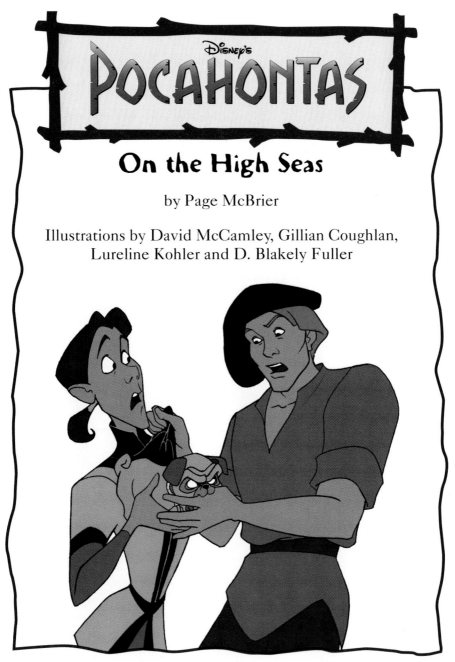

Grolier Books

Published by Grolier Books.
©1995 The Walt Disney Company. No portion of this book may be reproduced
without the consent of The Walt Disney Company.
Produced by Mega-Books, Inc.
Design and art direction by Michaelis/Carpelis Design Assoc., Inc.
Printed in the United States of America.

ISBN: 0-7172-8469-7

CHAPTER 1

Pocahontas sat on the riverbank dangling her feet in the cool, clear water. It was spring. All around her, the woods were filled with the colors of dogwood, redbud, and wild roses in bloom.

Pocahontas took a deep breath of the fresh air, then watched a heron take off from the water's edge. It sailed gracefully into the sky, long legs trailing, before it disappeared into the thick trees.

Pocahontas's thoughts wandered. What

would it be like to be able to fly up into the treetops anytime? What would her village look like from above? She imagined even Powhatan, her stern and powerful father, would look small from the heron's view at the top of the tree.

Pocahontas picked up her basket and sighed. There was so much she wondered about. All her life she'd lived inside the village. She wanted to know what was beyond her village.

Sometimes she wished she could be like her animal friends, Flit the hummingbird and Meeko the raccoon, who could come and go as they wished. If only she could explore by herself for as long as she wanted! What would she find? What sorts of adventures would she have?

Pocahontas felt a gentle hand touch her shoulder. "Psst! Pocahontas!" She looked up and saw her best friend, Nakoma, smiling at her.

"Where've you been?" asked Nakoma.

"You went out to gather berries when the sun was high."

Pocahontas stared down at her empty basket. "Has it been that long?"

Nakoma laughed. "You're always day-dreaming, Pocahontas."

"I can't help it," Pocahontas said. "I . . . wonder about things, that's all."

"Like what?" Nakoma asked.

Pocahontas shrugged. "I was imagining what it would be like to be a heron."

Nakoma sat down. "Why would you want to do that?"

Just then, Flit buzzed past Pocahontas's ear. He sped over to a blossom and took a long drink.

Pocahontas thought for a moment. "To see new things," she told Nakoma. Her eyes grew soft. "Do you remember once," she asked quietly, "when a friend of Father's came to our village? He told us stories about strange men with hair growing on their faces. He said they came from far away, from another place, but now they were here. They wore funny costumes and spoke a different language."

Nakoma laughed. "Everyone knows those stories are made up," she said.

"But what if they aren't?" Pocahontas persisted. "What if there really are hairy-faced men?" She gazed across the water. "If I could fly great distances like the heron, I could find out."

Nakoma rolled her eyes. "Fly like a heron? You? I doubt *that* will ever happen."

Pocahontas turned to her. "Maybe not. But something is going to happen. I can feel it." She eagerly leaned forward. "I keep having this strange dream, Nakoma. I don't know what it means, but it's about a spinning arrow. The arrow keeps going around and around and then suddenly stops and points at something. Only I can't tell what it's pointing at."

Nakoma shook her head and laughed. Then she stood up and brushed the dirt off the back of her skirt. "You and your dreams, Pocahontas! Who knows what they mean? Maybe the spirits are trying to tell you something."

"Maybe," Pocahontas answered.

Nakoma gently took the empty basket out of Pocahontas's hands. "Make sure you're home before dark."

"I'll be home soon," Pocahontas said. Her eyes drifted back to the water. Soon she was deep in her own thoughts again.

CHAPTER 2

While Pocahontas daydreamed, far out at sea a ship named the *Susan Constant* was heading for her country. On board were about a hundred men, all of them hoping to settle in what they called the New World. Many were farmers and craftsmen, but there were also sailors and adventurers aboard.

Up on the half deck, a soldier and adventurer named Captain John Smith was teaching his friend Thomas some unusual sailing knots he'd learned in his travels. Another settler, Lon, was practicing the hornpipe, a small instrument made of wood and horn.

John glanced over at Will, the young cabin boy. Will was carving another notch in a long wooden stick. "How many days now, Will?" asked John.

"Forty-two," he answered.

John stared out at the empty blue sky. "Forty-two days at sea."

"How much longer till we see land again, John?" asked Thomas.

"Don't know, Thomas," he answered. "I've never been to the New World. I don't expect it'll take much longer."

Thomas groaned. "I don't think I can stand another stale biscuit or piece of moldy cheese."

"There's worms in the barley gruel," Lon added, putting aside his hornpipe. "I counted three different kinds this morning."

"There's worms in everything,"

Thomas said. He closed his eyes and smiled. "What I wouldn't give right now for a piece of Mum's blackberry pie!"

"Mmmm," said Will, sniffing deeply. "How about a thick slice of roast beef with gravy? And some Yorkshire pudding?"

"Oh, it's not so bad, fellas," John said. "Look at the beautiful day we have here."

"About time," said Ben, a settler who had just wandered on deck. "It's been nothing but rain for the last eleven days. And it's so crowded below there's no place to move around."

Behind the men, the door to a cabin was flung open. John Ratcliffe, governor of the future colony of Virginia, stalked out. He was followed by his pug dog, Percy, and his manservant, Wiggins.

Ratcliffe approached the men. "What's all this chatter?" he demanded.

"Nothing. Just passing the time, Governor," said John.

"There's plenty of *that* to go around,"

Thomas added with a smile.

Everyone laughed.

Ratcliffe's eyes narrowed. "You think this is all fun and games, Thomas?"

"Oh, no, sir!" said Thomas. "On the contrary. I was just making a joke. It's nice weather for a change, and so—"

"You decided to be a comedian," Ratcliffe said, finishing the sentence.

Everyone became quiet. Thomas shifted his feet. Percy leaned around from behind Ratcliffe's legs and growled at Thomas.

"I've been informed," Ratcliffe said, "that our helmsman, Wilson, is still sick with the fever. That leaves us short one man on the third watch tonight." His eyes moved across the group and rested on Thomas. "Aha! The man who has lots of extra time. Thomas, you'll stand to the helm tonight."

Thomas was shocked. "Me? But I—"

John cut in. "Pardon me for interrupting,

sir, but Thomas hasn't had enough experience to stand to the helm. Why can't one of the seamen like George Martin do it?"

Ratcliffe looked at John impatiently. "It's time Thomas learned," he said. "We all have to pull our weight around here."

Ben hopped up. "But, sir! You want Thomas to learn to man the tiller on the night watch?"

"I told you," Ratcliffe repeated stubbornly, "he's got to learn sometime."

"But it will be dark, sir," John said.

The other men nodded.

Ratcliffe gave John a withering look. "I don't think he's going to *hit* anything, Smith. Do you?"

Behind Ratcliffe, Wiggins giggled. Ratcliffe spun around. "It wasn't meant to be funny, Wiggins."

Wiggins bowed deeply. "Sorry, sir. But you do exhibit a biting wit. Ha, ha."

Percy looked up at Ratcliffe and whimpered. Ratcliffe reached down and picked him up. "What is it, my precious?" he cooed. "Are you ready for your walk?"

Percy whined. His short fat tail wiggled back and forth.

Ratcliffe plopped Percy onto the deck. "Wiggins, take care of Percy."

"Yes, sir," said Wiggins.

Percy stuck his nose in the air and pranced past the settlers. As he went by Thomas and Ben, he growled.

"Same to you, pup," Ben said under his breath.

"Is there a problem here?" Ratcliffe snarled.

"Oh, no, sir!" Ben said. "Forty-two days at sea, and we're still happy as clams."

Ratcliffe smiled. "Good," he said. "I expect a happy group."

CHAPTER 3

That night a squall came up, surprising everyone.

John was asleep when he suddenly felt himself being hurled through the air. He slammed onto the floor, crashing into an iron-bound chest.

"Ow!" someone yelled. "What's going on?" In the darkness, men were being rocked and thrown about. Barrels and baggage slid back and forth.

"Must be a squall!" John shouted.

"Not again!" shouted another settler.

The *Susan Constant* pitched violently to the left and then to the right. Icy water began pouring down the ladder.

Wiggins stumbled down the rungs, wet and shivering. "The governor says all hands on deck!" he shouted at them. "And has anyone seen my umbrella?"

From above them, Ratcliffe's voice floated down. "Wiggins, are you keeping an eye on Percy?"

Wiggins's soggy shoulders slumped. "Yes, sir," he called back. "Right away." He disappeared up the ladder.

The ship continued to rock and pitch. Lon tried to light a lantern, but the jerking motion of the ship made it impossible.

Desperate cries were coming from above. "All hands on deck! Hurry!"

John spotted Ben and pulled him toward the ladder. "Follow me," he called. Together they climbed the slippery rungs to the space above.

Unsteadily, they made their way towards the helm.

The wind was blowing ferociously. The ship rolled from side to side. Thomas was clinging to the whipstaff, the pole that controlled the tiller. The pole jerked from left to right. Ratcliffe was shouting.

"What are you doing, you idiot?" Ratcliffe screamed at Thomas. "Can't you keep that thing still?"

Thomas's face was pinched in concentration. The pole jerked back and forth. "I'm trying to, sir."

"Ten degrees to starboard!" Ratcliffe shouted. "Can't you tell port from starboard?"

"I keep forgetting. Which is which?"

"Port is left, you fool! Right is starboard!" Ratcliffe snapped.

The ship leaned dangerously to one side and then to the other. "Are you trying to get us all killed?" Ratcliffe yelled.

Ben rushed over and grabbed the pole.

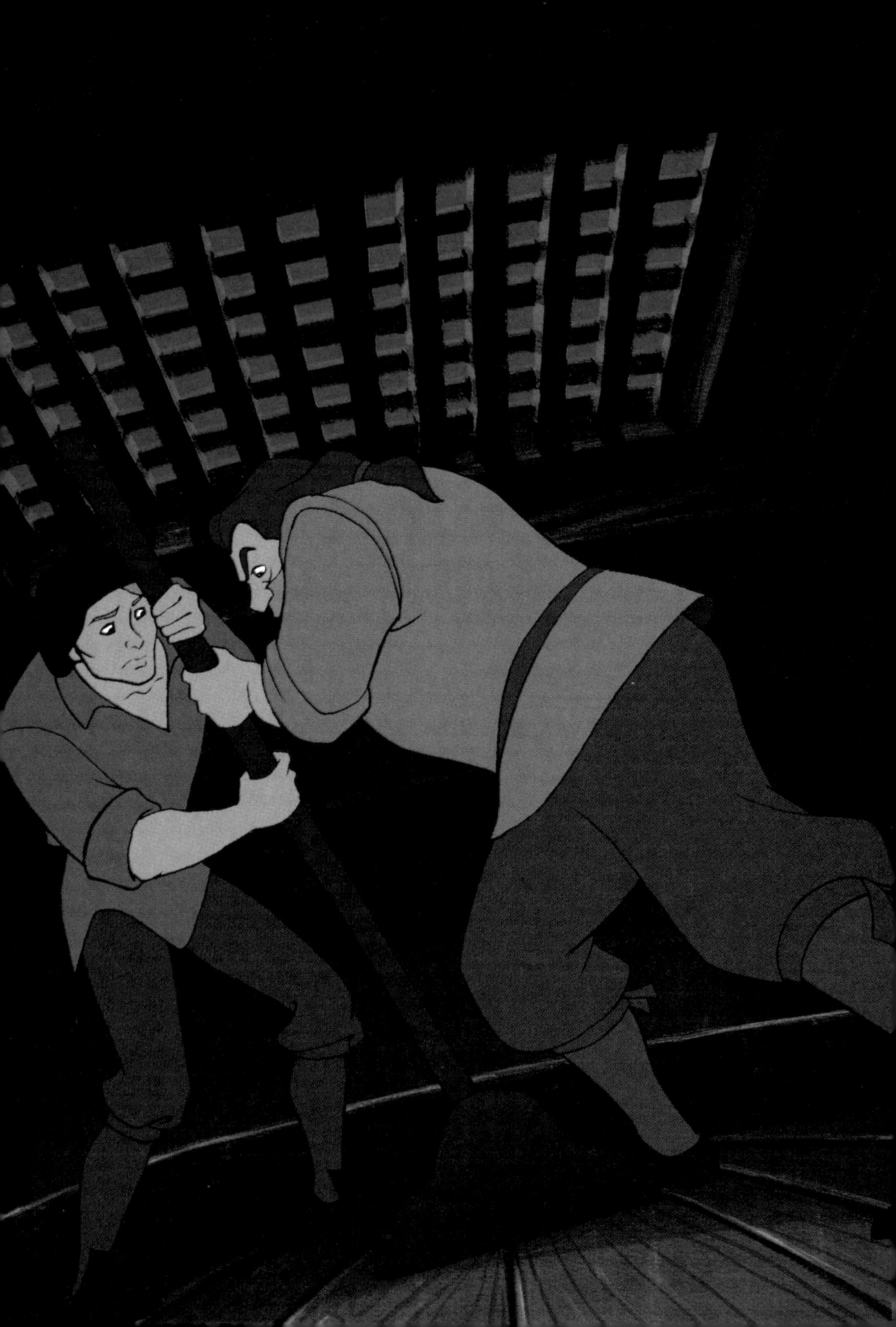

With all their strength, Ben and Thomas steadied it. Slowly the ship began to straighten up.

"I've got it!" Ben yelled.

Thomas's face filled with relief. "Thank you, Ben!" He stared angrily at Ratcliffe. "I don't know why he has it in for me," he muttered.

Above them, the ship's giant sails flapped noisily.

"Thomas!" Ratcliffe shouted. "If you're no use at the helm, go above and help Lon and the others furl the sails before they all rip apart." He began to bark orders to the other seamen as John and Thomas made their way up to the main deck.

When they got to the main deck, Thomas glanced up and gulped. Lon was slowly inching his way up the rigging, or ratlines, on the foremast. He looked as if he were hanging on for dear life as he climbed the shaky rope ladders.

Thomas glanced at John. "He can't be serious!"

"Thomas!" Ratcliffe shouted as he followed them on deck. "This is no time for hesitation. Get up there on the double. I need you to shorten the main topsail."

Thomas gasped. His face turned pale. "But, sir . . ."

The main topsail was high up on the ship's mainmast. Thomas would have to climb the ratlines up two enormous sails to get there. Then he would need to balance on a line just beneath the yard, the crosspiece the sail was tied onto, and pull up the heavy sail.

"Get going, Thomas," Ratcliffe ordered.

John shook his head in disbelief. "Governor," he said, "Thomas has never been into the rigging before. He's only a farm boy. You can't send him all the way up to the topsail. He'll be killed before he reaches it!"

Ratcliffe's face darkened. The wind

howled fiercely as the ship crashed into the oncoming waves. If they didn't lower the sails soon, they'd tip over.

"Fine, Smith. If you think Thomas needs assistance, then *both* of you can go."

Thomas turned to John, panicked. "Will you help me?"

John nodded. "Don't worry. We can do it. Just listen to me. I'll make sure you're okay."

"Hurry up, you two!" Ratcliffe shouted. "What do you think this is? A tea party for the queen?"

At that moment, Wiggins rushed out of Ratcliffe's cabin. Under one arm, he clutched Percy. In his other hand, he held his umbrella. "Look what I found, sir!" he exclaimed, cheerfully waving the umbrella. "Now I'm ready for this nasty weather."

A gust of wind blew past Wiggins. The umbrella turned inside out, throwing him off balance. He spun out of control toward the side of the ship.

"Watch out!" Ratcliffe yelled.

Still clutching Percy, Wiggins managed to grab the ship's railing just before he and Percy sailed overboard.

"You idiot!" screamed Ratcliffe. "You almost lost Percy."

Wiggins glanced miserably at Percy. Percy snarled.

In an irritated voice, Ratcliffe said, "Get Percy inside the cabin, Wiggins." Ratcliffe spun around angrily and faced Thomas and John. "And you two, get aloft."

Thomas started to take an angry step toward Ratcliffe, but John pulled him back.

"C'mon, Thomas," he said. "No time for that. We'll get through this." Hunched over, they made their way to the rigging and began to climb. They moved up slowly, hand over hand.

The ship pitched violently back and forth, and the rain pelted their faces. It was so dark they could barely see the lines in front of them.

Thomas tried his best to concentrate. As they climbed, John kept talking to him. "Hand over hand, Thomas. One rung at a time. That's good. Keep going. You're doing fine."

Then, just as Thomas reached for the next rung, the ship jerked to starboard.

"Help!" Thomas tried to grab onto the line, but in the darkness his hand missed the target. He fell through the air and hit the deck with a thud.

"Thomas!" John shouted. He scrambled back down the rigging and rushed to Thomas's side.

Thomas was out cold. His face was as white as the sails.

Several of the men stopped what they were doing and hurried over.

Will, the cabin boy, asked, "Is he all right?"

John lifted Thomas's wrist and felt his

pulse. "I think so," he replied. "Looks like he'll be all right when he comes to."

Ratcliffe appeared behind them. "He'll be fine," he bellowed. "Get back to work, men. Furl those sails!"

John pursed his lips. "Yes, sir." He signaled to Lon, who had made it up into the mainmast lookout post. "Wait there," he shouted. It didn't take John long to climb up and reach the lookout.

From there, he and Lon inched their way up the ratlines to the topsail yard. Clinging on tightly, they used a series of lines and pulleys to furl the sail.

Once that was done, John and Lon carefully made their way back down to the lookout. There they were able to furl the mainsail with the help of several other men.

The ship seemed to be rolling less. "We did it!" they shouted to the men below.

On the deck, Thomas had sat up and was rubbing his head.

"Are you all right?" asked John once they were on deck.

The color was returning to Thomas's face. "I think so," he said. His eyes fixed angrily on Ratcliffe.

CHAPTER 4

By the next morning, the sea was calm. Several seamen were up in the rigging, busily repairing the torn sails. The settlers, exhausted from the night before, were resting on the deck. Lon was practicing his hornpipe. Ben was next to him. A few of the other settlers were heating a small, dry piece of salt beef over some wood coals.

"Think that meat's going to taste any better now?" Ben called over to them.

"At least it won't be full of worms," George said. He was scraping the mold off a bit of Cheddar cheese.

Ratcliffe walked up briskly. "Good morning, crew." Unlike the others, he appeared neatly combed and groomed. Under his arm, he held Percy. "I trust everyone had a good night's sleep?"

"Yes, sir," one of the settlers mumbled.

Ratcliffe spotted Thomas resting on a big coil of rope. "Glad to see *you're* feeling better today, Thomas," he said with a slight smirk. "That was some fall."

"I know," Thomas said through clenched teeth.

"Still," Ratcliffe continued, "we often have to learn by experience. Although I'm not sure we wouldn't have been better off without you."

"Sir?" said Thomas.

Ratcliffe's eyes narrowed. "You almost sank us last night, you fool," he shouted. "What did you think you were doing?"

Thomas's face turned red. "I told you I didn't know how to man the helm."

"You didn't know how to do anything," Ratcliffe stormed. "The only thing you did well was fall."

Thomas bit his lip and stared at his feet. Everyone was quiet.

Ratcliffe tapped his foot on the deck, then sighed. "Well, at least the ship is under full sail once again—no thanks to you." He rubbed Percy behind the ears. "And my little Percy is safe and sound. Did you know he was so filthy from being knocked around that Wiggins had to give him a bath in fresh water this morning?"

Thomas looked up. "A bath, sir?" The settlers had to save whatever fresh water was left for drinking.

"Yes," Ratcliffe declared. "He smelled like a fish."

Percy sniffed and began to squirm in Ratcliffe's grasp.

Ratcliffe noticed the men heating the

salt beef. "What is it, Percy? Are you hungry again?" He fished around in his pocket and pulled out a piece of ham. He dangled it in front of Percy's nose. "This is the last one for today," he said. "You're getting too pudgy."

The men on the deck watched hungrily as Percy's jaws opened and shut on his juicy treat. Food was in short supply on shipboard, and each settler was allowed only a small amount each day.

Ratcliffe looked around. "Well," he snapped, "what is everyone staring at?"

The settlers turned their eyes away.

"And why aren't you men busy?" Ratcliffe barked. "There are plenty of repairs to make after last night's storm. Thomas, quit lounging around and make yourself useful for once."

Thomas stood up. Anger rose within him, but he controlled it and said, "What would you like me to do, sir?"

Ratcliffe waved his arm. "I don't know.

Think of something." He stormed off.

When he was gone, Ben pulled a piece of stale biscuit out of his pocket and angrily threw it down. It shattered on the deck. "Baths! Ham! Why should a dog be treated better than a man?"

"Because he's not just any dog," Lon said. "He's the governor's dog."

"Aw," said Ben with disgust. "We'd be better off without both of them."

Thomas gasped. "Ben! How can you say that? Ratcliffe is the leader of this expedition."

"True," said Lon. "And things will be different in Virginia."

"How?" asked Thomas, sitting back down.

"For one thing," Lon said, "there won't be differences in rank as there are now. Just because you're a farmer, Thomas, that won't make you less than a nobleman like Ratcliffe. We'll all be the same, man for man."

Ben scoffed. "You're dreaming, Lon. There will always be men like Ratcliffe to push us around. We should take a stand."

"Lon is right," Thomas said. "Where we're going, there'll be a new way of life."

"But Ratcliffe will be there, so how—" Ben began.

"What's this?" asked John, who was wandering past. He stopped and sat down beside Thomas on the coil of rope.

"Don't listen to Ben," said Lon. "He doesn't know what he's talking about."

Thomas shook his head and looked around at his friends. "Maybe he does. Maybe we have to take a stand against Ratcliffe."

John gently placed his hand on Thomas's shoulder.

Ben slammed his hand into his fist. "Right you are, Thomas. We've had enough of Ratcliffe's cruelty. It's time for a new leader."

"Mutiny!" Lon whispered darkly.

Thomas stood up.

"Keep quiet!" said John. "You're making a big mistake . . . ."

"No, I'm not," Ben said. "A new world calls for a new leader. Why should we listen to him?"

"Hear, hear!" said Thomas, clapping Ben on the back. "It's time for revenge."

"Thomas, you can't do this," John told him.

"Oh, no?" Thomas answered. "Just try and stop us!"

CHAPTER 5

That evening, a secret meeting was held in the hold at the bottom of the ship. Barrels of water, beer, salt meat, and other provisions were stored there.

The hold was an unfriendly place, even for sailors. It was damp, dark, and smelly.

Thomas, Ben, Lon, and several of the other settlers had gathered together. They sat huddled on some spare sails, with a single lantern overhead. Rats and cockroaches scurried past.

In a hushed voice, Thomas said, "No one must know of this meeting. The punishment for mutiny is death."

The other men nodded solemnly.

"Did you see Ratcliffe feeding his dog ham today?" asked George. "We've been told for weeks there's no good meat left."

"I saw Wiggins eating good Cheshire cheese and dried fruit this morning at breakfast," said another settler.

"Cheese! Fruit!" exclaimed another. "Why, the drinking water today was green. I counted three types of worms in it. And he's dining on good cheese and fruit?"

There was more grumbling among the men. "He's hoarding all the best food," said Ben finally.

"And besides that," said Lon, "he knows nothing about sailing. He should never have stood Thomas at the helm."

"Or made him climb the mainmast," said another.

"Right," said Ben. "I say it's time for us

to choose a new leader."

Lon spoke up again. "I've been thinking about what Ben and Thomas said this morning. Ratcliffe has to go."

Above them, the hatch to the hold creaked. The men looked up.

"Help!" Wiggins crashed down the ladder and landed in the middle of the men.

Percy tumbled down behind him. He leapt into Wiggins's arms, terrified.

"You!" shouted Ben. He jumped up and pointed a finger at Wiggins. "You were spying on us, weren't you?"

"Who, me?" said Wiggins. "Don't be absurd. We were on our way down here to look for . . . um . . . apples. Right, Percy?" He grabbed Percy and started edging his way back to the ladder.

"Liar!" said Thomas. He looked at the others. "Wiggins must have followed us down. I bet he heard every word."

"Who, me?" Wiggins repeated. "I never heard a thing. The word *mutiny* never

came up." Wiggins clapped his hand over his mouth. "Uh-oh. I mean, *monotony* was what you said, wasn't it? Boredom can be a terrible thing at sea . . . ."

"Get him!" shouted Lon.

"No! Help!" Wiggins clambered up the ladder.

"No, you don't," said Thomas, grabbing his ankles. "I know what you're up to. You're going right back to Governor Ratcliffe, aren't you?"

"Let go of me!" Wiggins yelled. He kicked his legs frantically.

"Never," said Thomas.

Wiggins dangled Percy in front of Thomas's hands. "Sic 'im, Percy."

Percy nipped Thomas's hand.

"Ow! Stop that!" Thomas yelled. He let go. Wiggins pushed Percy ahead of him and slipped through the hatch.

"After him!" shouted Thomas. "We can't let him get away!"

CHAPTER 6

The men took off after Wiggins, dodging barrels, trunks, tools, and cooking pots.

"What's going on?" someone called from a bunk.

"Save me!" Wiggins screamed. He tripped over a cooking pot but managed to hang on to Percy and keep going.

Startled by the noise, Will sat up. "What's happening?" he yelled.

Wiggins scooted around a table bolted to the floor and scrambled up the ladder.

"Don't let him get away!" yelled Ben, following Wiggins.

In the moonlight, Wiggins dodged an open hatch and ran toward the bow of the ship. The men raced behind. "Have mercy!" he yelled. He circled back and headed toward the stern.

Lon and Thomas tried to cut him off. "Over here, Ben!" yelled Thomas. "This way. Follow me."

They caught up with Wiggins, still clutching Percy.

"Aha!" said Thomas, grabbing Wiggins by the collar.

"We've got you now," said Ben, blocking his path.

"Don't hurt me," Wiggins pleaded. "I beg you! Can't we work something out?"

"Like what?" asked Thomas. He loosened his grip. Percy leaned over and opened his jaws. Thomas dodged, but Percy was too quick.

"Yeow!" Thomas screeched. "He bit

me again!" Wiggins let go, and Percy dropped to the deck. He and Wiggins took off again, this time in separate directions.

"Come back here!" yelled Ben, chasing them. With three quick steps, he caught up with Percy. "Gotcha!" he said, swooping down.

Percy's fat little legs paddled helplessly in the air.

"Lon!" called Ben. "Get Wiggins before he reaches Ratcliffe."

Wiggins was just about to knock on Ratcliffe's door when he heard Ben call his name.

"Oh, Wig-gins," sang Ben.

Wiggins stopped and turned around. Ben lifted Percy over his head. "Missing someone?"

Wiggins gulped.

The door to Ratcliffe's cabin swung open. Ratcliffe poked his head out.

Ben clamped one hand over Percy's

muzzle and stuffed the dog under his shirt.

Ratcliffe held up his lantern. "What's all the commotion out here?" he asked. The men were silent as Ratcliffe's lantern moved from one to the next. His eyes came to rest on Wiggins. "Wiggins, have you seen Percy?" he asked. "He isn't on his pillow."

"Uh . . . " Wiggins broke into a sweat.

"I told you to keep an eye on him," Ratcliffe said impatiently.

Wiggins nodded and wrung his hands. "Of course, sir."

"If anything should happen to him," Ratcliffe went on, "you're responsible." He turned on his heel and slammed the cabin door shut.

"Uh-oh," said Wiggins.

Ben yanked Percy out from underneath his shirt. "Whenever you're ready to make a deal, Wiggins . . . "

Percy's eyes bulged.

Wiggins frantically waved his arms.

"Wait!" he cried. "I can be reasonable."

Ben raised his eyebrows. "You can?"

"Oh, yes. Absolutely. Without a doubt," Wiggins babbled.

Ben nodded to Thomas and Lon. "Good. Then let's talk."

A hand clamped down on Ben's shoulder. "No, Ben," said John, stepping into the moonlight. "I think it's time *we* talked first."

CHAPTER 7

Ben took a step back. "Stay out of this, John," he said.

John put out his hand. "Give me the dog, Ben."

Ben shook his head. "Can't."

"Why not?"

"It's between me and Wiggins."

"I won't say anything," Wiggins begged. "Cross my heart. Just don't do anything to Percy. Please?"

"I don't believe that," said Ben. "The

minute I let him go, you're heading straight for Ratcliffe to tell him what you heard in the hold."

Thomas looked from Ben to John. "He's right, John," he said. "A few of us got together tonight and—"

John grabbed Thomas's shoulder. "Listen! All of you!" He glanced around to make sure no one else was listening, then said in a low voice, "Mutiny is a serious crime! The punishment is death."

"Better to be dead than under Ratcliffe's leadership," Thomas replied.

"No, you're wrong," said John. "Think about what you're doing. We'll be off this ship soon and starting out together in a new world. Think about what awaits each of you. Thomas, what about that big house you want?"

Thomas stared at the deck. "What about it?"

"Imagine! Your own land! Your own house! You wouldn't have had that in

England. You can work hard and get rich. Don't throw away your dreams because of a foolish plan to get even."

Thomas was quiet. Lon said, "It's more than that. Ratcliffe has been making our lives miserable for too long."

John went on. "True, he's a hard man. He can be cruel and impulsive. But think about what's ahead for us. Lon, I thought you wanted to open a blacksmith shop. In England, you would never have been allowed to do that. Your family are all farmers."

"I hate farming," said Lon softly. "I never did like cows."

"And what about you, Wiggins?" asked John.

"Who, me?" said Wiggins.

"Yes," said John. "You're hoping to find gold in the New World, right?"

"We'll be rich!" crowed Wiggins.

"You're already rich enough," snorted Ben. "You and this fat pug live like princes while the rest of us starve."

"Forget about that for a minute, Ben," said John. "What are you hoping to find in the New World?"

"Gold," said Ben. "Adventure."

"So you and Wiggins can *both* be rich. We can all be rich."

"I don't see what that has to do with our plans," said Ben. "I still say we get rid of Ratcliffe."

"I agree," said Lon. "He's gone too far."

Thomas, who had been listening quietly, spoke up. "Wait. I want to say something. Maybe John has a point."

"Don't listen to him," scoffed Ben.

"Maybe we shouldn't be so shortsighted," Thomas went on. "There's lots that can go wrong with a mutiny. What if the rest of the crew doesn't go along? What if Wiggins changes his mind and tells Ratcliffe before the mutiny starts?"

Wiggins tried to protest, but Thomas cut him off. "What if one of us got injured in the fight? I'd rather take my chances being wounded by an Indian."

"Right," said John. "Save the fighting for later."

Ben pointed an accusing finger at Thomas. "You're backing out, aren't you?"

"I'm only thinking things over," he said. "Soon we'll be on a new adventure in a new world. I can't forgive the way Ratcliffe treated me, but I'm willing to put it behind me now. And I think the rest of you should too." He turned. "Lon?"

"I agree, Thomas."

"Ben?"

Ben shook his head. "I don't like it. I still say we mutiny."

"Anyone else agree with Ben?" asked John.

There was silence.

From the lookout, one of the seamen called out, "Ten degrees to starboard!"

The ship swung slightly to the right. The sea stood calm, and the moonlight

fell evenly across the deck. Thousands of stars splashed across the sky.

"Come on, men. It's late," said John. He took Percy from Ben and handed him to Wiggins. "We've got another long day tomorrow." He looked Wiggins in the eye. "And you will keep quiet about this or answer to me."

Wiggins nodded and clutched Percy.

CHAPTER 8

On the riverbank, Pocahontas felt someone gently tug at her hair. She turned with a start.

"Nakoma!"

Nakoma held out Pocahontas's berry basket. It was brimming with juicy wild strawberries.

Pocahontas looked around. The sun had begun to dip down to the horizon. The air was growing cooler. "Has so much time passed?" she asked.

Nakoma laughed. "It's time to go, Pocahontas," she said. "They're going to wonder what's happened to us."

Behind Nakoma, Meeko poked his head out of the bushes. He sniffed in the direction of the berry basket, then stole over to Nakoma's side. Just as he was about to reach his paw into the basket, Flit buzzed down and cut him off.

Meeko squealed and tumbled backward down the riverbank. He landed in the water with a splash.

Pocahontas and Nakoma burst into laughter.

"Poor Meeko," Nakoma said. "Are you all right?"

Meeko scrambled back up the riverbank and shook the water out of his coat. Pocahontas smiled and reached into the basket. "Here you go, Meeko," she said, tossing him a handful of berries. "Tell Flit to stop being such a busybody."

But Flit had begun a noisy conversation

over the water with a passing sea gull. Flit listened for a moment and then buzzed back to Pocahontas and Nakoma. He circled Pocahontas's head.

"Now what is it, Flit?" she asked. "What are you trying to tell me?"

Flit zipped out over the water and back again several times.

Pocahontas and Nakoma laughed and shook their heads.

"Maybe he knows something about your dream, Pocahontas," said Nakoma.

Pocahontas sat quietly for a moment. Finally she said, "It's only the river, Flit. What's so different about the river?"

Flit circled around Pocahontas's head once more and flew off.

Pocahontas stood up. "Come, Nakoma," she said. "It's late."

The two girls chatted happily on their way back toward the village.

Behind them, the *Susan Constant* sailed into view.